Basil King

Going West

in large print

MEGALI

Basil King

Going West

in large print

Reproduction of the original.

1st Edition 2023 | ISBN: 978-3-38707-120-7

Megali Verlag is an imprint of Outlook Verlagsgesellschaft mbH.

Verlag (Publisher): Outlook Verlag GmbH, Zeilweg 44, 60439 Frankfurt, Deutschland
Vertretungsberechtigt (Authorized to represent): E. Roepke, Zeilweg 44, 60439 Frankfurt, Deutschland
Druck (Print): Books on Demand GmbH, In de Tarpen 42, 22848 Norderstedt, Deutschland

GOING WEST

BY
BASIL KING

1919,

GOING WEST

CHAPTER I

He was not a born fighter, in spite of a big, husky frame through which the urge of physical life was strong. On the contrary, he was a civilian and a business man in every nerve of his body. Eight generations on American soil had bred a type essentially industrious, notwithstanding all the fighting in which the family had been engaged. His father had fought in the Spanish-American War; his grandfather in the Civil War; his great-great-grandfather in the Revolution; farther back, his ancestors in the Connecticut Valley had beaten off the French and Indians for nearly a hundred years.

All that, however, had been alien to the main purposes of life. It had been incidental, not professional. Its chief influence on Lester lay in the assumption that, men being called for on the borders of Texas and in Mexico, he had no choice but to go. True, he was just beginning, after certain wayward years, to see success as a broker ahead of him; and within the month he had become engaged to Molly Dove. But these considerations could not weigh against the appeal of country, nor annul those traditions of duty that had come to him from the past.

So in the course of time, and with the march of events, he found himself in the enemy trenches, facing a burly blue-eyed Teuton holding a rifle by the barrel and swinging the butt about his head, while he himself held a bayonet in his hand. Amid the wreckage, the carnage, the tumult, he was desperately trying to recall his instructions as to how to stick the weapon in.

Before telling what happened then, let us go back and follow rapidly the stages by which Lester found himself in a situation which two or three years earlier he would have laughed out of the list of possibilities.

The son of a well-to-do bookseller in a great Atlantic city, he was an instance of that reaction against the paternal bent with which we are all familiar. His father was a gentle, scholarly man who loved books as books. The Spanish-American campaign had left him with one leg slightly shorter than the other, and the air of a retired general. All his longings had once focused themselves into the hope that his son would enter into, and one day inherit, a business built up on years of diligence and judgment—only to be disappointed.

Lester had no interest in books. He was not only an open-air fellow with a zest for sports, but he had all the inclinations of a genial, jovial soul. Taking wine, women, and song as kindred joys, he chose brokerage as the profession that would give him closest touch with the merry give and take of life.

As a broker he could steal all the time he needed to "root" at games, after he had ceased to play them actively, while the same career rendered him more free to marry a girl like Molly Dove, a waitress in the café where he generally lunched, to whom his family bitterly objected.

His mother was a small, square-shouldered woman, with a smile so bright that it was difficult for the most penetrating eye to see behind it. Lester had inherited her dark color, her beetling brows, and her vigorous physique. A gay audacity, as real as it looked, was also not the least among the legacies she passed on to her son.

Of his two sisters, Cora resembled the father and Ethelind the mother. Ethelind, too, had that gay audacity, the most patent result of which was to involve her in conflicting love-affairs. A wild-eyed thing, she was formed on that permanent-seventeen model that came in with the second decade of the twentieth century and induced all women, whatever their time of life, to dress as school-girls. Cora, tall, dignified, reserved, was the graduate of a woman's college, in which it was her ambition one day to hold a professorship. To sisters as well as parents the stalwart, wilful boy would have been the king among young men had it not been for his entanglement with Molly Dove. They could pardon his "wildness," knowing that it would pass, but they found it hard to forgive his choice of a wife in a sphere so much below him. In fact, they did not pardon it at all. In spite of his announcement that the engagement had become definite, no one responded to his invitation to make the acquaintance of the girl.

In the matter of his "wildness" there were already stirrings of a change of heart, though they hardly rose to the level of active consciousness. Such reforms as he made were avowedly in deference to Molly Dove. In cutting out—the term was his—women, wine, and song, he made it clear to himself that he did it, not in obedience to a moral law, but because "Molly asked him to." Molly held the odd conviction that such indulgences were wrong, chiefly because they came in between him and a great mystery, of which he had heard vaguely all his life, but from which instinctively he turned his mind away.

"There's really no mystery at all," she asserted, in that pretty way of hers which he found at once tranquil and enthusiastic, "no more than there's a mystery about the sun. When we fill the atmosphere with smoke we can't see it; but that doesn't keep the sun from being there. Blow the smoke away, and you find the sunshine as bright as ever."

He liked to hear her talk in that way, though he was not won by her beliefs. Far in the future he saw days when he would have shot the bolt of his temptations and settled down with her into being the "good fellow" she hoped to make of him. In the mean time—

But in the mean time came the call. It was the kind of call against which his instincts and his interests both rebelled, but he took it with no more analysis than he gave to the necessity of getting out of bed on a winter's morning. There was no help for it; it was all in the day's work.

His family took it in the same way. It was as much a matter of course as when Ebenezer Lester shouldered his eighteenth-century musket to defend the stockade against the Iroquois stealing down from Canada. It was as much a matter of course as when Charles E. Lester, the bookseller, rallied to President McKinley against Spain.

It was also a matter of course to Molly Dove. It would postpone the wedding for which she had begun her simple preparations, but she had a curious, secret facility for renouncing her own will. Her right-about-face was made with smiling lips and glistening eyes, and no effort that any one could see. To Lester she whispered:

"It's going to be all right, dear. Whatever the clash of human wills, there's only one real Ruler in the universe. The closer we can keep in touch with Him the nearer we shall be to the usefulness and happiness which make up what we call our destiny."

"That's all very well." He smiled, patting her hand. "But suppose I'm shot—or die of a fever?"

Her reply would have staggered him if he had not put it down to the sweet and charming eccentricity which made her different from other girls.

"Well, suppose it does happen that in the course of doing your duty this mortal should 'put on immortality'—that's the way the Bible expresses it, you know—wouldn't that be a gain for you? And what's a gain for you couldn't be a loss for us."

He laughed with a great guffaw. "But perhaps we shouldn't be married."

"No; but marriage, after all, is only for time, whereas you and I are bound by all sorts of ties which really belong to eternity."

He took no stock in that, he told her; but he liked her gleaming earnestness in saying it. The aunt who had brought her up must have been a quaint, religious character, he said, to have filled her head with such other-worldly notions. Anyhow, they were different from the anxiety and fear which the family hid behind their stoic calmness, and of which he felt the twinges within himself as he wound up his affairs.

CHAPTER II

It was at the time when the possibility of a war with Mexico—or any war at all—struck the imagination of the country as a calamity too horrible to contemplate. There was no question as to the victory, but neither was there a question as to the price that would be paid for it. Men—young men—young Americans, O God!—would be killed—actually killed. Fellows whose places were in shops and offices and factories and banks, whose diversions were the stadium, the sea-shore, or the woods, would be called on to make the extreme sacrifice at a time when sacrifice of any kind was being pooh-poohed. It was not only monstrous, it was unnatural, a trend of events in the teeth of fate, and against what one might reasonably call the manifest will of God. Lester knew that his family were feeling this, though they never mentioned it; he was feeling it himself. Molly Dove alone seemed to ride on the wave of events like a sea-bird on a storm, cradled, rocked, at ease in her element, secure, serene, sure of both present and ultimate good, whatever might befall.

So there came a Sunday when, after a mid-day dinner, the family accompanied him to the station and he entrained for camp. He had said good-by to Molly Dove during the forenoon. As no advance had been made to her from the Lester side, she could make none on hers, and so judged it wisest to keep out of sight. Her sweet self-effacement in doing this made Lester swear that he would marry her at the first opportunity, as he steamed away on this opening stage of what was to prove his long, long, long way.

That way, at the beginning, struck many people as a tortuous, futile way, leading no-whither. There was talk of saluting the flag; there was the occupation of Vera Cruz; there was the withdrawal from Vera Cruz; there were months when the daily head-lines bore the names Huerta, Villa, Carranza; and few knew for what reason the young men did not come home.

Then home they began to come, chiefly on furlough, to be sent elsewhere. During one such interval Lester married Molly Dove. It meant a breach with his family, none of whom appeared at the simple ceremony or took any steps to acknowledge the bride. He was compelled to leave her within a month.

In the mean while greater wars than any possibility with Mexico had broken out, and the iron entered the whole world's soul. It was only then that the end of the road on which Lester had started out that Sunday when he had entrained came into sight—and he sailed for France.

His life after that could scarcely be distinguished from hundreds of thousands of other lives. One overruling need had bound the manhood of the race into a solidarity so tense that the individual was swallowed up in it. Lester was no longer a son, a brother, a husband, the father of a coming baby; he was an infinitesimal part of a huge machine, with no more to say in matters of his life and death than the wheel to the man who turns it round. He could only turn; he could only turn as he was told; he could only turn as millions of other wheels were turning, without volition, without knowledge, and, to a degree that surprised him, without much preference or choice.

In minutes when conscious of himself he could see how little he was the Lester of other days. When he woke up in the morning it was often with a strange, dull wonder as to what he had become, and how and why he had become it. It was like a rebirth—only it suggested a rebirth into hell. In fits of moral nausea, after some phase of a "good time," at any date within the past ten years, he had called down on himself some such fate as that; but he had never looked for it so literally, and right here on earth.

The inevitable came at last. By stages such as have often been described, he found himself in that section of the trenches known to its occupants as Dead Cow Lane. Life there was much as he expected it to be, though possibly not quite so bad. Its worst feature was in the long, dull hours it allowed for thinking. He loathed sitting on the fire-step with nothing but a slouch, a grouch, and the wit of his mates to keep him company. All that was humanly repulsive he learned to endure; but when he lounged idly on the fire-step, one leg swung across the other, and a dead cigarette between his lips, he ate his heart out. Molly, waiting for her baby, in a tiny apartment with a kitchenette, was a vision against a background of eyes that seemed to watch for him. His father's were grave; his mother's steely; Cora's earnest; Ethelind's wild. They looked down at him, right there in Dead Cow Lane, in a vigil that made him frantic. When the command came at last to go over the top it brought with it not only terror, but a break in the monotony.

What happened then was also along the lines he had been prepared for. So many tales had been told him, and he had listened with such eagerness that, from the minute of going up the death-ladder, he seemed to have been through it all before. Everything went as if it had been rehearsed. He had the lonely feeling on finding himself in the open other men had described to him. As he ran through the lanes of barbed wire his agony of haste was neither more nor less than theirs. The "p'—p'—p'—p'—p'—p'" of the machine-guns; the crackling of bullets through the air; the tottering and falling of his comrades, throwing up their arms and tumbling clumsily on backs or faces, were all as if by rule. He had no more consciousness than that. He was neither brave nor afraid; he was only numb. It was something to be done, and he was doing it. He might have been doing it in his sleep—in a nightmare.

On reaching the German trench, which the barrage fire had crumpled into a welter of earth, cement, timbers, uniforms, dead and wounded men, and pots and pans, he practically tumbled in. There was no horror in the minute, because horror has its limits and this had passed beyond them. A wounded German was crawling away to anything that would shelter him, and in order to scramble up Lester had to step on the man's head. The head gave way, with an oath or a groan, but Lester managed to keep his feet. All round him there was shouting and yelling and cursing, and now and then a demoniac laugh. Every American was trying to kill his German, and the Germans were at bay. Lester, too, was trying to kill. The infection had caught him. Out of the blank, out of the numbness, out of the paralysis of the spirit in which he had run across No Man's Land, something surged up of which he had no time to take account. It didn't wait for him to take account of it. It seized him with a maddening pang—a hate to which he had never supposed his nature could be equal—a hate welling up from the depths of his subconscious self—a hate of the enemy—a hate of the German—a hate of the very first individual who came his way—with a wild accompanying frenzy to stick his bayonet in a heart. "Give 'em hell," were the words with which he had been sent over, and all his life and all his longings and all his love were fused in one red flame to deal out hell as it had been dealt out to him.

How he found himself face to face with a big, blond Bavarian, whose blue eyes danced with a kind of bloodshot fire as he swung the butt of his rifle like a club about his head, there is no way of telling. It was one of those instances which war supplies by the million in which world-rancors, race-rancors, and the suppressed irritations of thousands of years sum themselves up in the hearts of two men who have no personal quarrel and who have never set eyes on each other before. It was like an unescapable destiny. The American broker and the peasant-actor of Oberammergau had been projected toward each other by an irresistible fate. Behind each were all the generations of rivalry and covetousness and savagery and sin that had sent him forth. Neither was moved by his own impulse. Each was but an instrument of the passions of the past.

Lester was not sure whether or not he saw double—whether or not there were two Bavarians swinging the butts of their rifles, or only one. Those who told the story afterward were in similar doubt. Some declared for two; some for one only; some saw three or four in that corner of the trench. In any case Lester had found his man; and no emotion he had ever known was half so sweet as this anguish of pain to get him.

Those who told the story afterward laughed as they pictured Lester dancing this way and that to avoid the descending club and slip his bayonet in under it. He dodged, they said, as if he were on springs. Time and time again the Bavarian seemed about to sweep him with a blow to the other end of the trench—but no! Lester was prancing as nimbly as ever, watchful, alert, his aim always at the heart. No one could tell how long this went on, for all observation was crazed. The only thing known for certain was that in the end Lester got his weapon in—and in—and in—to the hilt— to the heart—and that if he had had time to go through the thick body he would have done it.

He didn't have time, and it was here that the testimony was in conflict. One man paid that the Bavarian was able to deal a last blow with superhuman strength. Another declared that a second Bavarian dealt it. Of those who came back some supported one of these assertions, and some the other; but there was no difference of opinion at all on the point that Lester's skull was cracked with a sound like that of a breaking egg-shell. His body and his opponent's lay tumbled together in a fierce embrace—the one with a surprised horror in the wide-open blue eyes, while the other—but they only said of Lester that his face was "all bashed in."

CHAPTER III

Lester's face was "all bashed in," but Lester himself didn't know it. The last thing he remembered was the queer, soft, mushy feeling as his bayonet pierced the Bavarian's uniform and entered his body. His next sensation was that of an emotion, a confused emotion, of sorrow, pity, or disgust.

At first it seemed all that had survived. He himself was safe—somewhere—and the Bavarian had died. He didn't try to move, or open his eyes, or seek to find out to what place they had carried him; he was too comfortable for that. But— a man toward whom he had no enmity on his own account, who was also perhaps a husband, with a little wife waiting for a baby in an apartment with a kitchenette, that man lay dead, with his, Lester's, bayonet wound in his heart. He was sorry. He remembered his hate; he remembered his passion to kill; he knew it as a blend of all the vengeances that had been stirring in his blood since Belgium had been invaded, and the *Lusitania* had been sunk, and the awful things had begun to pile upon the awful things; but it was a vengeance that began to seem to him beside the mark. It was the kind of revenge man didn't know how to take; the kind of justice he didn't know how to mete out. The innocent were being punished for the guilty, as if a child were hanged because a man had committed a crime. He couldn't say that he reproached himself for his part in that; he knew he had been acting on orders from above; but he was conscious of a deep

16

regret that the world should have grown so stupid that such things had to be.

Otherwise he was resting. He supposed that he must have been wounded, though he could feel no pain. Oddly enough, when he tested himself for pain he didn't know where to begin. But it was his own immunity, his sense of well-being and security, that sent his thought the more persistently toward the man he had kept from ever returning home.

Trying to fancy what that home was like, he found himself, suddenly but naturally, in a village street, of which the bordering houses, of plaster and timber, had low roofs and picturesque eaves. All round there were mountains.

"This is Oberammergau," he heard in a language he understood. "Here is my home. Let us go in."

They entered without the opening of doors, coming into a room with rafters, small windows, and an air of antiquity. A woman was kneeling beside a bed above which hung a carved wooden crucifix. On each side of her knelt a quaintly dressed child, with hands stiffly pressed together.

"That is my wife," said the voice. "Those are my children. They're praying for me and asking that I shall come home."

"Should you have liked to go home?"

It seemed natural to Lester to ask this question. Everything seemed so natural that he had not yet reached the point of inquiring how it had come about. The Bavarian reflected.

"I should have liked it before knowing what this is. I should like it even now, for their sakes. But since death has to be destroyed in us one at a time it's better for us to be here, don't you think?"

Lester began to be startled. "Here? Where?"

"Wherever it is we are. I don't quite know where that is. Do you? I'm speaking," he continued, "in the old terms of place in the sense of locality, because I don't know what else to do; but locality, of course, is gone. We're in the universal, which makes it difficult for us, after being used to so many limitations, to understand ourselves."

Lester was aware of fear, awe, and irritation all struggling in him together.

"You may be in the universal, as you call it; but—but I've come through."

"We've both come through. The marvel is that we've done it so easily. It's as I expected—only more so."

"As you expected—in what way?"

"Every way; all my life. When your barrage fire began I prayed—"

"Do you fellows *pray*?" Lester asked, in astonishment.

"Oh, some of us—what we used to call prayer—the sort of thing my poor wife and children are doing now—begging—pleading that this or that shall be done—instead of resting in strength, as you and I are."

"I'm not—I'm not—resting in strength."

"Oh yes, you are! You are, without knowing it. It's what human beings are always doing. They get every kind of good in their lives, and don't know the source from which it comes. You won't know to what your present actual comfort is due till—"

But the woman rose from her knees, and so did the children. Wiping away their tears, they began the preparations for a frugal breakfast. As Lester felt the presence that had accompanied him moving from his side and enveloping all three in tenderness, he found himself alone with his thought again.

There was no shock to him in the fact that, as Molly had expressed it, the mortal had put on immortality; he had faced the possibility for too long. Ever since the first entraining he had accepted it as an eventuality of war. On sailing for France he knew there were increased chances against his ever coming home. In the months that followed he grew accustomed to death and more or less obtuse to it. He smoked and chaffed is the morning with fellows who by noon had gone—who could tell where? They used the euphemism of "going west"—into the sunset, into the glory, into the great repose. It was the easiest thing to say, and many a time he had said it of himself. "By this time next year I may have gone west." Then it became: "By this time next month I may have gone west." Later it was: "By this time tomorrow—" "Within an hour—" "Within half an hour—" "Within ten minutes—" as the seconds slipped away.

Well, he had gone west! The odd thing was that he had done it so easily, so painlessly. The tedious hours in the trenches faded more or less from recollection. The going over the top and all that followed after it became nothing but a blur. Even the months in camp, in Texas, behind the lines in France, dissolved like vapors when they mount into the air. What was present to him most forcibly was the thought of the dear ones he had left behind.

His own conditions were entirely a matter of course; he was perfectly at home in them. Though he could not have described them, nor have given an account of them, he knew that they were pleasant and that they were profoundly rooted in nature. He was neither surprised at them nor unduly curious.

Neither was he lonely. His sufficiency was such that companionship as he had always conceived of it was not a consideration. The condition in itself was companionship to a degree he could not understand. It was vibrant with life; there was speech in it. Had he been forced to make explanations, he would have said there was intelligence in it, and comprehension. He let himself sink into the enjoyment of it as a baby rests without questioning in the love by which it is enlapped. No; he wasn't lonely; he didn't know what loneliness was.

But he felt care—the care for Molly, the fear of the blow that would fall on his father and mother and sisters. Now that he knew what had happened, his thought fixed itself on finding some way by which he could help them.

On this point he wondered why, if the Bavarian could return to his home and whisper something of comfort, he could not return to his. Distance was not a factor, since it was no part of the universal. Even the gulf between the material and the non-material could in a measure be crossed. Why, then, could he not cross it?

"Is it because I've been such a bad fellow?" he asked himself.

"Not entirely," the Bavarian answered, as if the words had been addressed to him. "It isn't a question of what we've done so much as it is of what we know. It's a matter of thought, of consciousness. When we've learned that everything exists in a great mind, that mind itself becomes the medium of intercourse. Give up the idea that the people you love live in one sphere and you in another. We all live together in one great intelligence that understands all our needs. Meet your needs not by your own efforts, but by co-operation with that intelligence, and what you want will be done."

Lester reflected on that. "What do you mean by co-operation?"

"Trust, in the first place—till trust becomes knowledge."

"But if this intelligence knows already what I need—?"

"It will do the wise thing, only you won't be associated with it. What you want is the association, to have your part. You don't get your part, you don't have the association, because you isolate yourself. Your mind is closed to the powers and activities that are all about you. When you understand what they are you will have your share in them."

"But why should my mind be closed if yours is open?"

"It's a matter of habit. We go on here from the very point at which we left off there. I had the habit already. Our life at Oberammergau bred it into one. You didn't have it. Your thoughts were limited to a physical world and a physical body and a physical way of doing everything. Now you have it all to learn, very much as you had in your physical childhood."

"Then I'm not being punished for my sins?"

He asked the question in some uneasiness.

"You are. Don't you see? The punishment is that you're not more advanced. You've been like the idle boy in school; and now you find it hard to catch up. If it were not for the great thing you've done you'd be farther behind than you are."

"The great thing I've done? I don't understand you."

"Every good act helps us onward; and among things that are good love is the greatest. Of that you've given the highest proof there is."

Lester was astounded.

"I?"

"You gave the most precious things you had—your business, your happiness, your family, your wife, your life. You held nothing back. You not only gave without reserve, but you gave without complaining. You didn't do it for yourself, but for a great cause—as men conceive of causes—and you did it of your own free will."

"And so did you."

"No; I waited to be taken. If I hadn't been taken I shouldn't have gone. I didn't offer myself up; I was seized against my will. You were the more like Jesus of Nazareth, Who laid down His life for His friends, and so, as He said Himself, losing your life you have found it."

"Oh, but I didn't do it in that way at all," Lester protested.

"It doesn't take anything away from right that we do it as a matter of course. We don't have to know the infinite intelligence to have the infinite intelligence know us. Isn't it a case of 'He that doeth the Will'? If we do the Will instinctively we can't fail of the protection of Him whose Will is done; and if we don't know Him already we can be sure He will make Himself known."

Communication once more came to an end, not abruptly, but by natural cessation, because the thought had been expressed.

But Lester was left with a clue to follow, and little by little he followed it. The immediate gain was a new kind of perception. It was as if some faculty already possessed, but paralyzed within him, had been freed. He could not have said that this endowment existed in hearing, or sight, or any of the senses, or in all of them together, or in none of them. All he could say was that it gave him a new use of power, of power to which he had a right, but of which, for a reason that escaped him, he had hitherto been deprived.

CHAPTER IV

As with this power there came freedom, expansion, and growth, he found himself able to reconstruct out of thought the house he had formerly called home.

He was back in it all at once—without effort, without coming from a distance, without journeying through space, without meeting the discords between timelessness and time. He was simply there, walking about the rooms and halls as he had done ever since his childhood.

He judged it to be evening, for his father was at home. It was what he, Lester, had wanted. His appeal was to be for Molly, that the family should pity her, should take her in, should make her one of themselves, and help her through the time that was ahead of her. He knew his appearing might be a shock to them, but it would be a shock to his father least of all.

The father was seated in the dining-room, reading a book by an electric lamp. When the supper was cleared away, he could have this room to himself. It was a cheerful room, with deep-red curtains drawn, and a deep-red cloth on the table. Lester entered without journeying through space, much as he had been in the habit of entering all his life. His sense of presence, of vitality, was so strong that he wondered his father did not look up.

"Father!"

But the father kept on reading.

"Father!"

There was no indication that he had been heard.

He went nearer. He placed himself where he must be seen. He spoke with more force.

"Father! I want to talk to you about Molly."

The father turned a page. Lester could hear the rattle of the paper. He could hear the little cough when his father cleared his throat. He could see the dark shade in his father's cheeks which showed he needed shaving. There was nothing about that well-known face obscure or unfamiliar; but he could make no sign of his coming that could be recognized.

Presently Cora came in and sat down. She began to talk about the book in her father's hands. To Lester it was like something on the stage, something done by human beings, but not part of life's reality. It struck him for the first time that mortal happenings pass in a realm of illusion.

From the fact that Cora was in colors he inferred that the news from France had not yet reached them.

"Cora," he said, "I want to talk to you about Molly."

"Oh, it's interesting enough," Cora admitted, in response to something said by her father, "especially the first part; but so trivial. If the dead really do live again I should think they'd find some better occupation than playing with a ouija-board."

"A ouija-board," the father argued, "might be only the simplest means they can find of getting their messages over."

"Then, since they're so limited in what they can do, why shouldn't they tell us something worth our knowing, when they've got the opportunity? This boy"—she waved her hand toward the book—"does no more than describe the same old life on earth—with variations."

"But perhaps with variations they live the same old life on earth."

"Then I don't want to believe in it." Cora's manner was decisive and professional as such manners are depicted by actresses. "As a matter of fact," she summed up, "the more I think, and the more I read, the less I'm inclined to accept a life beyond the grave as a possibility. Such books"—again she indicated that in her father's hand—"express a natural human yearning, as do also the myths of the New Testament, but—" She left her sentence there. The father, too, left it there, as if at heart he agreed with her.

27

"I wonder where mother is," Lester asked himself, and immediately was in her room upstairs.

She was seated before a mirror, trying on a hat. Another hat was on a chair beside her. Two bandboxes with a disarray of silver paper stood beside her on the floor. Ethelind, short-skirted, and moving with nimble, sylphlike feet, was standing back to get the effect.

"I think I like that one the better of the two," she was saying, "and yet I don't know but—"

"Oh, they're awful, both of them," the mother complained. "It's funny I can never get a hat that suits me but the same old thing."

Lester went forward. He meant that she should see him first in the mirror. The reflection would startle her, of course, but he should be able to reassure her.

It was he who was startled first, since, standing before the mirror, he didn't get his own reflection. He felt so solid, so warm, so full of energy, that it seemed to him impossible that a reflection should not be cast. But there was nothing—nothing but the image of his mother casting her bright eyes up at the cockatoo crest on a hat that suggested a Mephistopheles.

"Mother, I want to talk to you about Molly."

"Oh, dear, what an old hag I'm beginning to look!"

"Oh no, you're not, mother dear," Ethelind returned, cheerfully. "That's just worry. One of these days the war will be over and he'll be coming back a great general—"

"What's the use of the war being over and his coming back a great general, when that creature will have the first say in him?"

Ethelind came behind her mother, to give the hat a twitch to a more effective angle.

"Mother dear, I don't believe he'd like to have you talk in that way."

Lester appealed to his sister.

"Ethelind, I want you to help me. I want you all to think of Molly. I'm not coming home; but I'm well and happy. That is, I could be happy if I only knew that she was being taken care of and that you were good to her."

But Ethelind only twitched the hat again, and the subject dropped. As it did a curtain seemed to come down on the scenes that had meant home to him, once more suggesting the action of a play.

There followed for Lester a further phase of unfolding thought, though with no solution of some of his perplexities.

"But it's always so," the Bavarian explained to him. "We can go to them more easily than they can come to us. The spiritual can to some slight degree re-embody the material; but spiritual things are only spiritually discerned. Jesus of Nazareth after His Resurrection could at times reincarnate Himself before His disciples; but they could not spiritualize themselves so as to follow Him when He disappeared. That can only be accomplished in proportion as they lay off the mortal and temporary by degrees, or burst out of it with a bound, as you and I did."

And yet in Lester's consciousness the vibrancy of life in his surroundings grew more tense. It was as if he were rising and ever rising on a mounting wave of vitality, but always riding on the top. Something like this energy he had felt in running, or rowing, or swimming, or on horseback, or in one or another of the sports in which he had excelled; but never with this joyousness of strength. The physical had given some sign of it, though it had been no more than as the single note of a shepherd's pipe to the fullness of an orchestra, or as the tramp of a lone step to the onrush of a million men.

And in one such swelling, exultant, glorious moment he came where Molly was in her little living-room in the apartment with a kitchenette. She was sitting at a table, with two or three books before her. One of them was open and to it from time to time she dropped her eyes. She raised them soon again to look straight into the air, as if she saw beyond walls into the reality where he was. There was no trouble in her eyes, nor sorrow, nor anxiety. In every feature there was peace, with the look of expectation.

He did not try at once to enter into communication with her. It was enough for him to study the pure face with its expression of repose. But he followed her thought as her eyes fell to the page of the book again. It was as if he were reading the words himself:

"And if Christ be not raised, your faith is vain; ye are yet in your sins. . . . If in this life only we have hope in Christ, we are of all men most miserable. But now is Christ risen from the dead, and become the first fruits of them that slept. For since by man came death, by man came also the resurrection of the dead."

She lifted her eyes and reflected on that. He drew nearer, bending over and about her.

"Molly, I'm here."

He saw her expression brighten. It was almost as if she had said, "Yes, I know."

"I want you to know, darling, that I'm not coming home."

Whatever was passing through her mind, she nodded, though no shade fell on her bright face.

"I'm well," he continued. "You must think of me as happy and as taken care of."

Again there was that nod, as if she assented to something she had heard. Presently she began to read again:

"Then cometh the end, when he shall have delivered up the kingdom to God, even the Father; when he shall have put down all rule and all authority and power. For he must reign, all he hath put all enemies under his feet. The last enemy that shall be destroyed is death."

"That enemy is destroyed, Molly. I've proved it. There's no death; there's nothing but life. There's not even a shock, or a minute of unhappiness. There's nothing but life, and then more life, and then life again. I was never so alive as I am at this instant, or so capable of doing things. Except for you, Molly, sweet one, and the baby that's coming, and the family, I wouldn't go back."

If her eyes grew grave it was with thought and not with foreboding. She returned once more to her book:

"For this corruptible must put on incorruption, and this mortal must put on immortality. So when this corruptible shall have put on incorruption and this mortal shall have put on immortality, then shall be brought to pass the saying that is written, Death is swallowed up in victory."

"Yes," he said to her, "that is what has happened to me. Death has been swallowed up in victory. If strength and energy and safety and joy constitute victory, then I'm victorious. If it were not for you, O my love—"

But she closed her book suddenly and rose. As she did so he could hear the words she uttered, almost aloud.

"I must do that," she said, with determination. "It's what he'd like. I must take it on myself."

CHAPTER V

He lost her for a while, and when he saw her again she was in the open air. He was with her, though not exactly by her side. As far as he could judge he was both leading her and following after her. He was above her, and also holding her hand. If he could have been everywhere about her at one and the same instant, it was that.

It seemed to be Sunday. There was no work going on in the streets, and there was the Sunday air of leisure. Molly walked rapidly, her eyes toward the ground. Her whole little figure expressed concentration of purpose.

He knew the suburb. The shady streets, the trim green lawns, the low stone walls with vines tumbling over them, the wooden houses painted for the most part in dull tones of red and yellow, were those with which he had always been familiar. High on a knoll he saw the deep verandas of his own old home. Molly did not hesitate. She turned in at the gate.

There was a short driveway, between clumps of shrubbery and under elms. At a sudden turning she met Ethelind. The two girls stopped and looked at each other as they came face to face.

"You're Ethelind, aren't you?" Molly said, without trembling or awkwardness.

Ethelind's wild eyes were all ablaze.

"Yes, and you're Molly. I'm—I'm so glad you've come. I've wanted to know you. I was coming one day to see you—I don't care what any one says. I know it's what my brother would want me to do. We—we miss him so."

"Thank you," Molly said, with a gentle smile. "I'm glad you thought of me so kindly. Just now there's something I want to say to your father or mother. Do you think either of them would see me?"

Ethelind's face fell.

"I—I can't say—for sure. They're—Oh, I don't know!—But my brother—"

"Yes, I know all that; but this is something important."

The girl seized the sister-in-law's arm. "It—it isn't—anything you've—you've heard?"

"It's nothing I've heard; it's only something that I feel I know."

But they had been seen from the window. The mother came running out, all her gay audacity transformed, as a lamp is transformed when, instead of giving light, it becomes the center of conflagration.

"Oh, what is it? What is it?" she cried, as she hurried toward them.

"It's nothing very definite, Mrs. Lester," Molly replied, calmly. "It's only something I feel so strongly that—"

"Oh, feel!" Mrs. Lester exclaimed, impatiently. "Don't frighten us with feelings when—"

"Is Mr. Lester in? I should like to talk to him as well."

The mother led the way toward the house. Molly followed, Ethelind clinging to her arm. It did not occur to any of them that no farther explanation had been made as to who Molly was. That seemed to take itself for granted.

The father was in the hall at the foot of the stairs. Cora was coming down them. Both had been summoned by the sense of something wrong. Molly went straight to her husband's father.

"Oh, I want to tell you, Mr. Lester; I feel I have a message."

"Feel you have a message?" he echoed, with a kind of tremulous severity. "What do you mean by that?"

"I don't know what I mean; only this morning he—he seemed to come and stand beside me—"

"Nonsense!" It was Cora who said that, from the position in which she had come to a standstill half-way down the stairs. To Molly she seemed very magisterial and commanding. "Nonsense!" she repeated. "This is pure nervousness—or hysterics."

"No, it isn't, Miss Lester," Molly contradicted, not rudely, but with imploring earnestness. "I'm sure he did come. He spoke to me. *Something* spoke to me."

"Did you hear anything?" the mother demanded.

"No, it wasn't in words; or if it was in words it was only as it turned itself into words in my own mind. It was more like—like a conviction—an intense conviction—that came to me from outside."

"And what did your conviction say?" Cora inquired, icily.

"It said— Oh, you must forgive me!—I shouldn't come if I didn't feel it so strongly!—It's as hard for me as it is for you—"

36

The father backed away to the baluster. His face had grown gray. The mother dropped to a hall chair. Ethelind was crying already, but standing by as if to give aid. Cora was still commanding and severe. It was she who interrupted.

"Yes; we understand all that. But tell us what you've come to say."

Under this authority and severity Molly began to grow nervous. She clasped and unclasped her hands, sometimes twisting her fingers.

"You see, it was this way. I was reading the Bible and— and thinking—and trying to understand what it meant— when all at once he—he seemed to be with me—and to be saying things."

"What sort of things?"

"I don't exactly know, Miss Lester. I knew he was there— and that he was telling me how beautiful it was with him— but I can't explain how he made me understand it—"

"No," Cora interrupted again, "nobody ever can explain. Once they get notions into their heads, they seem to think explanations are not important." She came down to the second lowest step, but still stood over the trembling young wife in her attitude of authority. "This is all nerves, my dear—and excitement. The book you were reading—oh, yes, it's a very good book, and full of the wisdom of the ages and all that!—But it reacted on you in such a way that you've conjured up these frightening things—"

"But I'm not frightened at all," Molly burst out. "That's the wonderful part of it. If he hadn't come and told me beforehand, and made me feel how happy he is, I should have been. But I'm not now; and I don't want you to be. That's why I came."

"Yes; no doubt," Miss Lester agreed, coldly. "But now that you've come, you'll do well to run home again and try to calm yourself and be sensible. If my brother has been"—she stumbled at the word, but forced herself to utter it—"if my brother has been—k-killed—we shall hear of it from the proper authorities."

"Cora, that's not fair," Ethelind cried, indignantly. "Molly's come over here to warn us, and even if she's wrong—" She broke off to make another sort of appeal. "Father, can't you say something? Here's your son's wife—the mother of the child he's expecting—"

But Mrs. Lester rose, still clinging to her chair.

"If this is a ruse for getting into our house and making our acquaintance whether we would or no—"

"Mother, how can you?" came from Ethelind. "You deserve that your son should never be given back to you. Father, can't you say anything at all?"

But what the father did say was uttered brokenly. "I don't—I don't believe it. He's not—not dead. She's come here to get us to own her—to take her in—"

"And if we don't," Ethelind cried, "and she goes away again, I'll go with her. Whether he comes back or not I shall be there."

It was extraordinary to Lester that he could look on at this scene without conscious pain. It Was exactly as if he had watched them rehearsing a play in which emotions were simulated but not experienced. When the rehearsal was over they would become their actual selves again. Beyond hardness, and suffering, and misunderstanding he could see the end.

He could see the end as Molly cast an imploring look around her and prepared to depart. Ethelind, who was already in street clothes, gave all the signs of going with her. Over them both Lester threw the protection of his love, which apparently gave them nerve. Neither of them flinched; but it was in Molly that the real valor shone. She was both quiet and firm as she took her few steps toward the door, Ethelind clinging to her arm.

But at the door there was a ring, and on the porch outside there stood a boy with a telegram in his hand.

"Charles E. Lester live here?"

Ethelind seized the envelope, while with feverish fingers Cora signed for it. The father took it in his hands and held it helplessly.

The mother uttered one great cry.

"Open it!"

He opened it—read it—and let it flutter to the floor.

Cora snatched it up; but she, too, dropped it after a hurried glance. She stood as if turned to stone.

The mother took it—sat down deliberately—read it carefully—read it again—read it again—and folding it, slipped it into the bosom of her gown.

Molly and Ethelind had not waited. They had not needed to hear the news. Rather they were eager to run away. It was Molly, however, who pressed onward, dragging the other with her—out to the porch—down the steps—on to the driveway.

The three in the hallway remained as if paralyzed, without tears, without words, seemingly without thoughts.

The mother came first to the possession of her faculties.

"Stop her," she cried, in a deep, tragic voice a little like a man's. "Stop her. Bring her back." She struggled to her feet, hurrying toward the door. "She's my dead son's wife. He

40

spoke to her. He's not dead. He's alive. If he wasn't alive he couldn't have come to her. Stop her. Call her back. She's my child. Nothing shall take her away from me."

Lester saw the two girls pause, while Ethelind whispered:

"Go back. She's calling you."

Slowly Molly turned round. Slowly she mounted the steps of the veranda. The vision faded out as Lester saw his mother's arms go round the neck of his young wife and draw her close.

But it faded out in radiance. It also faded out in confidence. He was not only at peace, he was at peace with the certainty of a vast readjustment.

It was readjustment in himself first of all—the adaptation of the "fan" at ball-games, and of the broker of The Street, to the eternities of which he could just discern the beginnings.

Then it would be the readjustment of his family—to each other—to Molly—to their memory of him. A new kind of tenderness would settle down among them with a new and farther outlook.

It would be the readjustment, too, of his country—to a new world-position—to a wider world responsibility. In the ending of enmities it would play a ruling part.

And it would be the readjustment of nations to nations, and of men to men. The blind hatreds that had hurled him against the Bavarian and the Bavarian against him would cease. Their folly would be recognized. Of the blood that had been shed, and was still to be shed, this would be the recompense. It would be shed to its highest purpose when it should be shown that it had been shed in vain.

Soon those who were in the turmoil that mortals create for one another would have come west like himself—into the sunset, into the glory, into the great repose. They would come into the great activities, too, where work never ceases, and strength never tires, and love never wanes. And as he turned into the radiance he felt content to wait patiently for that.

THE END

CONTENTS